THE MIDWICH CUCKOOS

ORIGINAL BY JOHN WYNDHAM

RETOLD BY PAULINE FRANCIS

D1628181

Evans

Published by Evans Brothers Limited
2A Portman Mansions
Chiltern Street
London W1U 6NR

© Evans Brothers Limited 2005
First published 2005

Printed in Hong Kong

Francis, Pauline

The Midwich
cuckoos / retold
by Pauline
                    JF

1566355

Copyright © John Wyndham, 1957
First published in Great Britain by Michael Joseph, 1957
This edition published by arrangement with Penguin Books Ltd
The moral right of the author has been asserted.

British Library Cataloguing in Publication data
Francis, Pauline
        The Midwich cuckoos. - (Fast track classics)
        1.Science fiction 2.Children's stories
        I. Title. II. Wyndham, John, 1903-1969. Midwich cuckoos
        823.9'14[J]

ISBN 0 237 52689 1

THE MIDWICH CUCKOOS

Introduction

John Wyndham was born near Birmingham, England, in 1903. When he was young, he tried many careers, including farming and law. He also began to write short stories.

In 1946, Wyndham left the army after the Second World War. He decided to try writing science fiction because he admired books such as *The War of the Worlds*, by H.G. Wells, and *Journey to the Centre of the Earth*, by Jules Verne.

The Midwich Cuckoos was published in 1957. This tells the story of a group of children with golden eyes who were born to the women of Midwich village after a strange day when everybody fell asleep – children with strange powers who terrified the village.

John Wyndham wrote many other well-known books including *The Day of the Triffids* (1951), *The Kraken Wakes* (1953) and *The Chrysalids* (1955). Many of them have been made into films.

John Wyndham died in 1969.

My name is Richard Gayford. My wife Janet and I used to live in the village of Midwich, an ordinary little village where nothing ever happened. She was the luckiest woman alive because my birthday was on the 26th September and we were away from Midwich when something terrible *did* happen.

I wrote many reports for Military Intelligence in the months that followed. This story is based on them and other events that happened years later. Friends gave me some of the information and the rest I saw with my own eyes...

CHAPTER ONE

A Sleepy Village

Janet and I stayed in London for the night of my birthday and drove back to Midwich on the morning of the 27th September. When we turned from the main road towards the village, we came to a ROAD CLOSED sign. A policeman held up his hand to stop us as an army lorry thundered towards Midwich.

"Army manoeuvres," he said.

We drove back to the main road and I pulled into a field a few yards further along.

"This is all very odd," I said to Janet. "Let's walk across the fields and find out what's going on."

We set off. I was a few yards behind Janet when it happened. As she walked on, she staggered and fell to the ground without a sound. I ran towards her, but I did not reach her. I, too, fell to the ground and I don't remember any more.

I woke up surrounded by soldiers and an ambulance man. A fireman was unfastening an enormous hook from my jacket. Then he threw the hook across to Janet and began to pull her towards me. She opened her eyes and sat up.

"Feeling all right, Mr Gayford?" a voice asked. I looked up and recognised the face of Alan Hughes, an army officer whom I had met in the village. He was the boyfriend of Ferrelyn Zellaby who lived at Kyle Manor in Midwich.

"Yes," I replied, "but what's going on here?"

"We don't really know yet," he replied. "It could be some sort of gas escape. You won't be able to get home yet. I suggest you book a hotel in Trayne for tonight and wait for the all-clear."

We thanked Alan and walked back to the car, none the worse for our little sleep. The inn at Trayne, the nearest village to Midwich, was crowded with newspaper reporters and army men. To my surprise, I met an old friend, Bernard Westcott. We had been in the army together.

"We're waiting to get home to Midwich," Janet told him.

"You *live* in Midwich?" he asked, staring at us thoughtfully. "That is why I'm here. To find out what happened last night. You might be able to help, Richard. How about coming into Midwich with me?"

I agreed and we set off soon afterwards.

"How much do you know about what happened last night?" I asked him.

"All the telephone lines went dead just after ten o'clock," he said, "and two houses caught fire. This morning, all the streets are empty." He looked at me. "Everybody – and everything – is asleep."

"But why?" I asked. "Was it an accident? Was it a gas – something to do with the army manoeuvres?"

"Nobody knows," Bernard replied. "An army aircraft has taken a photograph of Midwich. It shows a pale, oval shape close to the centre of the village. The affected area – where everything fell asleep – stretches for two miles around it."

We passed through the road block without any difficulty and climbed to the top of a hill overlooking Midwich. The army captain positioned there took out a map. On it he had drawn a large circle with the village church almost at the centre.

"Whatever this shape is, it has no smell," he explained. "It hasn't moved. It doesn't show up on radar. It sends you to sleep straight away, but has no serious side-effects. We won't know any more until we take more photographs tomorrow."

"We have to keep this quiet," Bernard said. "I've told the reporters it's an army mistake."

But no more photographs could be taken. By the next day, the shape over Midwich had disappeared and people in the village were beginning to wake up. The village soon returned to normal and the strange experience was called the Dayout.

"It will be very important to keep an eye on the village in the weeks to come," Bernard told us as he was preparing to leave Trayne. "You two could help me."

"You're asking us to spy?" Janet asked coldly.

"No," he replied, "but I want to make sure that Midwich is... well, safe. You don't think it was an accident that the newspapers didn't get hold of the real story, do you?"

"No," I replied, "I don't know what's going on, but I realise it's top secret. We'll do what we can to help."

"What are you expecting to happen here, Bernard?" Janet asked.

"We don't know what this thing is, or does," he replied. "But we *have* to watch what happens."

I soon had plenty to report.

CHAPTER TWO

Keeping the Secret

A few weeks after the Dayout, Ferrelyn Zellaby was coming downstairs for breakfast at Kyle Manor. Her father, Gordon, was already working in his study.

"I've *got* to tell somebody!" she thought. "If Angela is at breakfast, I'll tell her now."

Angela, Ferrelyn's stepmother, was still at the table. Ferrelyn ate some cereal, but pushed her egg away. "I was sick this morning," she announced.

"So was I," Angela replied.

"I think I was sick because I... I'm going to have a baby," Ferrelyn said.

"Me, too," Angela replied. She began to cry. "Sorry, my dear!" she said, "but I'm so happy."

"I'm frightened," Ferrelyn said. "It's different for you, being married."

"Alan will marry you," Angela replied. "He loves you. You *must* tell him."

"But you don't understand!" Ferrelyn wept. "It wasn't Alan! It wasn't anybody! That's why I'm so frightened."

During the next few weeks, so many women visited Dr Willers because they were expecting babies that he went to ask Gordon Zellaby for help.

"Something strange is happening," Dr Willers said. "There are so many unexplained pregnancies in the village that the vicar and I think it has something to do with the Dayout. Some of my patients are not married. Many are young girls or women who have *never* had a boyfriend."

"How many women?" Zellaby asked.

"All the women in the village who are able to have children," the doctor replied. "About sixty-five in all. The married women have accepted it – but as for the others... We've got to say something, even if it upsets them."

"How much should we tell them?" Zellaby asked. "Should we let them find out for themselves?"

"Find out what?" the doctor asked. "No, you're right, Zellaby. This is a mystery, isn't it?"

"*How* it happened is a mystery," Gordon Zellaby said, "but *what* has happened is not. I... " He suddenly stopped. "Good God!" he said at last. "Angela and Ferrelyn, too!" He pushed back his white hair and smiled grimly. Then he stared at the carpet for a minute in complete silence. "As far as I can see, there is only one explanation for what has happened. These babies have been planted inside them. The women in Midwich are being used as hosts to grow something... a child... that is not theirs."

"We must call a meeting for all the women," Dr Willers said. "Do you think Angela would be willing to speak to them, as one pregnant woman to another?"

Gordon Zellaby nodded. "We must do all we can to make them less anxious," he said.

All the seats in the village hall were full on the night of the meeting. Angela Zellaby sat on the platform between Mr Leebody, the Vicar, and the doctor. Mr Leebody stood up.

"I beg every one of you to listen carefully to what Mrs Zellaby has to say," he began. "Dr Willers and I will wait in the next room, but we will return afterwards to answer any questions you may have."

They left. Angela Zellaby took a sip of water and began to speak. "I must warn you that what I have to say will be difficult for you to believe," she began. "I am going to have a baby. I am delighted. But, unhappily, there are many women in Midwich who are also expecting babies who will not be happy at the news." She stopped speaking and looked around the hall. "Something very strange has happened in Midwich."

The women sat silent, their eyes fixed on her. A woman called Miss Lamb tried to speak but her friend, Miss Latterly, told her to be quiet. "I object to what you have said about the women in our village," she shouted at Angela. "I shall leave at once. And so will Miss Lamb."

But Miss Lamb did not move. She looked away from her friend, her face blushing red. Miss Latterly grew pale, lifted her head high and left the hall alone.

"We are not to blame," Angela Zellaby went on. "It will be worse for those women who do not have the love of a husband to help them through this. And I think you will agree that this should be Midwich's secret. We do not want the newspaper reporters to pester us. We must all protect the children we are going to have."

Angela looked at the women in the hall. Nobody spoke. A few were crying quietly.

"I shall now ask Dr Willers and the Vicar to come back in," she said at last.

She slipped into the little room where they were waiting. Zellaby guided her to a chair where she leaned back, pale and exhausted.

"I'll be alright," she said. "I know what those women are feeling, Gordon. We've got to answer their questions, let them get over the first shock before they go home. We must help each other. I need it, too. It isn't true, about being happy. It was, two days ago, but it isn't now. I'm frightened."

He put his arm around her shoulders. "It's going to be alright, my dear," he said. "We'll look after you."

"It's not knowing *what* it is!" she replied. "I only know that something is growing inside me. It makes me feel like an animal."

Gordon Zellaby kissed her cheek. "You're not to worry," he said. "When the time comes, we'll face it together."

CHAPTER THREE

Golden Eyes

The meeting was a great success. The women began to feel that they could get through their ordeal if everybody helped them. A committee was formed to organise social activities to bring people together. Life appeared to be running smoothly, until the Vicar's wife disappeared.

A few days later, the Vicar of Trayne brought her home. "I found her preaching in the market place," he said to Mr Leebody. "She said she was being punished for her sins along with all of Midwich. She said you were suffering here from a... a plague of... well, babies. Then my wife saw that your wife was pregnant. That will explain it, I'm sure."

In mid-March, Alan and Ferrelyn, who were now married and living in Scotland, came to visit Midwich. Angela had not explained anything to them in her letters, but now it was time for them to learn the truth. They listened in silence. It was Ferrelyn who spoke first.

"You know," she said, "I had a feeling all along that something was wrong. How terrible! And Alan was forced to marry me!"

"This is a shock, sir, isn't it?" Alan said to his father-in-law when the two women had gone into the kitchen.

"I'm afraid it is," Zellaby agreed. "But the shock does wear off, I'm pleased to say. But for the women, this is only the first hurdle."

"It's going to be hard for Ferrelyn," Alan said, "and for you and Angela."

"Do not underestimate my daughter," Zellaby said. "And try to stay calm for her sake."

"I'm amazed that Midwich has managed to keep such a secret," Alan said.

"So am I," Zellaby admitted. "Even the nearby villages have no idea of the number of babies we are expecting in the village."

Throughout May, the tension in Midwich increased day by day. Then something happened which raised everybody's spirits. Miss Lamb went out for an early evening walk, slipped on one of the milk bottles outside her cottage – and five hours later, the first Dayout baby was born. Dr Willers came home late after delivering the child. His wife was waiting up for him.

"Charley. Charley, my dear," she said. "Was the baby…?"

"Perfect. Just perfect. Nothing wrong at all," he replied.

"Thank God for that," she said.

"It's got golden eyes," he told her. "Strange. But there's nothing wrong with golden eyes, is there?"

"No, dear, of course not," his wife replied.

"All that worrying!" Dr Willers said, "and now it's

perfect. I…I…" He burst into tears and covered his face with his hands. "It's perfect, except for the golden eyes. I'm so tired."

A month later, Gordon Zellaby was pacing up and down in Trayne's maternity hospital. Ten minutes later, a nurse came in. "It's a boy, Mr Zellaby," she said. "And Mrs Zellaby has asked me to tell you that he has the Zellaby nose – and blue eyes."

On a fine afternoon in the last week of July, Gordon Zellaby saw a family coming from the church as he left the Post Office. One of them, a young girl, was carrying a baby.

The Vicar greeted Zellaby warmly.

"All the mothers are having their babies baptised," he said. "Young Mary over there chose the name herself. Theodore. It means "Gift of God." The fact that she is not ashamed is a tribute to everybody in this village. Teamwork, that's what this village has had – led by your wife."

"But that young girl has been robbed of her childhood," Gordon Zellaby said. "She has suddenly been forced to grow up. No chance to stretch her wings. That makes me sad." He paused. "I hear that your wife is coming home soon," he continued. "How is she? Is the baby well?"

"Yes," Mr Leebody replied. "She adores it. But *who* are these children? There's something about the way they look at you with those strange golden eyes. They are… they are strangers."

"I hope that we did the right thing," Zellaby said. "To have strangers among us."

CHAPTER FOUR

Home Again

A few weeks after all the babies were born, I sent this report to Bernard Westcott.

Dear Bernard

I am writing to you urgently. A strange thing has happened. My friend, Gordon Zellaby, was the first to notice it. His daughter Ferrelyn, who recently had a Dayout baby, turned up at Kyle Manor. He was surprised because he did not know that she was coming to visit. She looked very pale and tired. This is what she said: "The baby *made* me come back."

The next day, I heard that four of the women who work at the research headquarters based in the village, and who were still away on maternity leave, had been forced by their babies to come back to Midwich. Miss Polly Rushton came back from London, too, with her baby, to seek help from her uncle, Mr Leebody. She had been visiting him during the Dayout.

Everybody is saying the same thing, Bernard. The government must make plans for the care and support

of these Children.

    I enclose reports from the doctor and Janet.

Yours,

Richard

Dear Mr Westcott

All the Dayout babies born survived – 31 males and 30 females – and all have these special features. Most unusual are the eyes. They are unique, being bright gold. Their hair is very soft and dark blond, and each strand, under the microscope, is flat on one side, and curved on the other, like the letter D. The fingers and nails are narrower than usual. Their skin has a silver sheen.

It is wrong that nobody is making a study of these Children. I am keeping notes, but they are merely a doctor's observations. Experts should be doing it. Something must be done before it is too late.

Dr C. Willers

Dear Bernard

I have read the above reports with great interest. I am writing to you because I feel very strongly about the events that Richard has described.

Dr Willers thinks that the women are returning with their babies because they are anxious. He thinks they want to be with the other mothers whose babies are the same as theirs. They know their babies are not quite normal and being with the other mothers makes them feel better.

I do *not* agree with him. All the mothers agree that the babies *force* them to do things. Ferrelyn said it was like feeling anxious all the time and only coming back here took the feeling away. Even Miss Latterly said so. She had to bring Miss Lamb's baby back for her because she was too ill to come herself. As soon as she left it with her neighbour, Mrs Brant, the anxious feeling went away.

And it's not just the women. Mr Harriman lost his temper and slapped his baby. Then he turned up at Dr Willers' surgery with a broken nose, two teeth knocked out and two bruised eyes. Two of the village boys said they had seen him hitting himself with his own fists.

I feel very strongly about this and have told Dr Willers that I am writing to you. I am angry because he would not include this information in his report.

Best wishes,

Janet Gayford

CHAPTER FIVE

Cuckoo Children

Bernard Westcott came back to Midwich as soon as he received our reports. He went to speak to Gordon Zellaby. Then he came to our cottage, looking very thoughtful.

"Your reports to me have been very good, Richard," he said, "but I wonder if you have been fair about Gordon Zellaby? I know he talks too much, but he understands what's going on more than most people. He doesn't agree with Dr Willers that the mothers who have come back are suffering from hysteria."

"Why not?" I asked.

"You mean you didn't know?" he replied. "Ferrelyn tried to take her baby for a drive in her car the other day."

"What do you mean, "tried"?" I asked.

"After about six miles, she had to give up and turn back," he replied. "The child doesn't like it. This is serious, Richard. It is wrong for a mother to be at the mercy of her own child. Zellaby wants something to be done about it."

It soon became clear that none of the Children liked to leave Midwich (we were by now using a capital "C" so that they would not be mixed up with the other children in the village). It was a nuisance for the mothers, but most of them did not think it was very serious – except for Gordon Zellaby. When his son-in-law came to visit, he decided to speak to him about the matter. He put out chairs on the lawn where they could speak without being disturbed.

"I would feel happier, Alan, if you could get Ferrelyn away from here as soon as possible," he said. "The sooner the better."

Alan looked at in him surprise. Then he frowned. "I want her to be with me more than anything," he replied. "She set out to see me once, remember?"

"I know," Zellaby said. "The baby brought her back, just as it brought her here before. We can arrange to have the baby looked after in the village."

"You mean, you don't believe that it's just hysteria?" Alan asked.

Zellaby shook his head. "I don't understand what it is," he said. "It could be a form of hypnotism. But whatever it is, it comes from the child. Try to help Ferrelyn decide. Remember one thing, it isn't your baby, and it isn't hers. These sixty-one golden-eyed Children are cuckoo children. And whatever happens next, it will happen because they don't want to die."

"What are you expecting to happen?" Alan asked.

"I don't know," his father-in-law replied, "but I don't think it will be anything pleasant. The cuckoo survives because it is tough. That is why I want you to take Ferrelyn away and keep her away."

"What if your child had been one of them?" Alan asked.

"I should do the same," he replied.

Angela came across the lawn. "I've just had one of the research workers on the telephone," she said. "She's left Midwich – and she hasn't taken the baby. She's refusing to let it wreck her life any longer."

"What if the other women follow her example?" Zellaby asked. "Who will pay for the Children to be raised in Midwich? And where will they live?" He turned to Alan. "You must get Ferrelyn away. Go and talk to her now."

Alan got up and walked over to the house.

"Cuckoos are very determined survivors," he told his wife quietly. "When a nest becomes infested with them, there is only one thing to do."

"You mean…?"

"I do, my dear," he replied. "These cuckoo children are dangerous. If you wanted to destroy the human race, you could just launch a weapon. Or you could use a more subtle weapon, one that you could use to attack from within – like the Children."

CHAPTER SIX

An Interesting Experiment

The next few months saw a few changes in Midwich. Dr Willers took a long holiday. In November, a 'flu epidemic killed three of the Children – two of the girls and Ferrelyn's son. But the most surprising thing of all was the sudden closing of the research headquarters. Everybody went, leaving behind four golden-eyed babies for whom foster parents had to be found.

A week later, a couple called Freeman arrived to live in the village. They were both doctors – and he had a special interest in psychology. It was their job to study the Children. They did this carefully, lurking around the village or sitting on the village green, watching.

"Who are they?" I asked Bernard.

"Nothing to do with me," he replied. "But I believe they are here because of Dr Willers' report. He was anxious for the Children to be studied."

"They could learn so much more if they were more friendly," I replied. "Let's hope they will be useful. I have to say, that except for not wanting to leave the village, the Children have caused few problems so far. They seem very sensible and close to each other – apart from wanting their own way."

But the following summer, when the Children were about a year old, Zellaby forced our attention to something new. He turned up at our cottage one sunny afternoon.

"This is important," he said, when I said I had too much work to do, "I must have witnesses."

"For what?" Janet asked, impatient.

"An experiment," he replied, "on the Children. Which one will it be first?"

"Mrs Brant's," Janet replied. "But he's hardly a year old."

We went to Mrs Brant's house and she led us to the boy. Zellaby gave him a little box. He rattled it and tried to open it, but he couldn't.

"What was the point of that?" Janet asked.

"Patience," Zellaby replied. "Now we'll try it on another boy."

This child played with the box. Then he held it out to Zellaby and waited. But he did not take it. Instead, he showed the baby how to open the box.

"Now we'll go back to the Brant child," he said.

The Brant baby took the box and opened it immediately, as if he had done it a dozen times before. We visited three other boys and they all opened the box. He repeated the experiment with the girls with the same result. We went back to the cottage for tea.

"I don't understand what you're trying to do," Janet said.

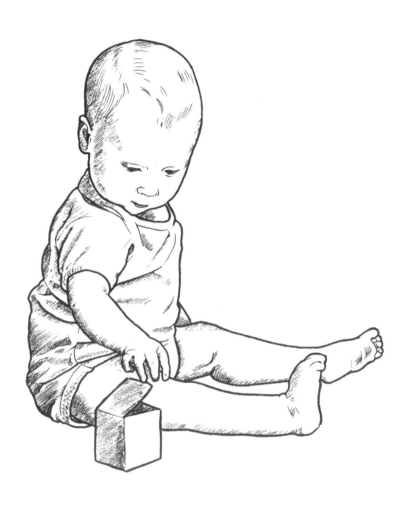

"I think you do," he replied, "and so does Richard. Don't be afraid to admit it."

"I suppose that your experiment shows that what one of the Children knows, all the Children know," I replied.

"Are you saying that if I told one of the Children something, all the rest would know it?" Janet asked.

"Certainly," Zellaby replied. "And the other question is this – does each child have a mind of its own? We seem to have fifty-eight individual bodies with only two individuals – *one* boy and *one* girl."

"I find that hard to believe," Janet said.

"In a way, insects have come close to this," Zellaby replied. "Think of ants. They cannot grow any bigger, so they have formed colonies which all work together. Even humans often combine in groups to work and live more efficiently."

It *was* hard to believe what Zellaby said. And to my relief, a few days later, I was offered a job in Canada.

"Thank goodness we're leaving," Janet said. "I've had enough of Midwich and I don't care if I never hear about the place again."

I did not return to Midwich for eight years, and then it was only because I bumped into Bernard Westcott when I was on holiday in London. Of course, I asked him about Midwich, half-expecting to hear that all the fuss had died down.

"I'm going down there tomorrow, as it happens," he replied, "to investigate the death of one of the village boys, Jim Pawle. His car crashed into a wall. Why don't you come with me?"

I accepted. I'm not sure why, and in that way, I found myself back in a horror I could not have imagined.

CHAPTER SEVEN

Murder on the Road

Bernard and I set off after breakfast on a fine summer's day.

"The biggest change in Midwich is the research headquarters," Bernard explained as he drove. "It's now a Special School run by the Ministry of Education. It's called Midwich Grange."

"For the Children?" I asked.

He nodded. "Zellaby was right in some ways, you know. When he was two, one of the boys learnt to read simple words and it was discovered the next day that all the boys could read them. It was the same with riding a bicycle and swimming. But most people believe they just have a way of sending thoughts to each other, rather than the group working as one person."

"Has the school been good for them?" I asked.

"Yes," he replied. "And most of the Children decided to go and live there. Their loyalty to one another is far greater than their loyalty to their families. Just one boy and girl attend a lesson on one subject and the rest know it instantly."

"They must be mopping up information like blotting-paper," I said. "And is their existence still really a secret to the outside world?"

"Yes," he replied. "The villages around think that Midwich Grange is some sort of mental hospital. Everybody knows the Dayout affected the Children. Everybody thinks they're just different."

Midwich looked exactly the same. The inquest decided that Jim Pawle had been driving carelessly because he had hit one of the Children. As he tried to drive off, he hit a wall. Accidental death. Afterwards, we were talking to Zellaby when two of the Children walked past. I stared at them in astonishment.

"Surely, those can't be... " I began.

"They are," Zellaby replied. "Didn't you see their eyes?"

"But they can't be!" I said. "They're only nine years old, but they look at least sixteen!"

"Come to Kyle Manor and have some tea," Zellaby said.

As we sat on the lawn, Zellaby turned to me. "The verdict was wrong," he said. "I saw exactly what happened that day. I passed four of the Children just before the accident. They were walking in a line right across the road. Jim Pawle wasn't travelling very fast. He did his best but he couldn't avoid them."

"That's when he hit the boy?" I asked.

"Yes. And then the car sprang forward while Pawle was still trying to brake. It smashed straight into that wall and burst into flames," he replied, his hands shaking. "I looked at the Children. They just stared at the wreck. There was no expression on their face at all. It was… it was deliberate murder."

"You mean that the Children did it?" I cried. "They *made* him drive into that wall?"

"Yes, just as they made their mothers bring them back to Midwich when they were babies," he said. "If anybody harms or angers the Children… it could be any one of us at any time. We've already sent our son away, and Angela may follow. For the last few years we have been living on the slopes of a volcano."

We said goodbye and Bernard drove us very carefully away from Kyle Manor. On the road, we passed four Children, two boys and two girls.

"Can you stop for a moment, Bernard?" I asked. "I want a closer look at them."

The likeness between them was even stronger than I had expected. They all had the same dark-golden hair, narrow noses and rather small mouths. I had forgotten how unusual their eyes were. They looked like glowing gold. The Children passed us without a glance or word. I found them disturbing and I was not surprised that their families had been happy for them to move to Midwich Grange.

Suddenly, a loud noise made us both jump and one of the boys fell to the ground. The other boy turned and looked at us, his golden eyes hard and bright. I felt weak and afraid. But at the same moment, another explosion came from behind the hedge and a loud scream filled the air. The boy's eyes left mine and turned towards it.

The boy on the ground moaned. The others began to moan, too. Then down the lane from the school swept a loud moan which mingled with those in front of us – a high-pitched piercing sound. We stood still, frozen by fright.

Six boys ran down the lane and carried the boy away. Bernard and I climbed into the field and found a boy lying on the ground, a gun under his body, his head bleeding. A young girl sat by his side, weeping.

"They've killed David!" she wept. "They killed Jim. Now they've killed his brother. I tried to stop him. I knew they'd kill him, but he wouldn't listen to me. He fired at the boy. Then he turned the gun round and shot himself."

I went back to Kyle Manor to use the telephone.

"The police will say that David Pawle committed suicide to avoid punishment," Zellaby said, when I explained what had happened.

"The way that boy looked at us!" I cried. "I didn't believe you before, Zellaby, but I do now! For a moment, he thought one of us had fired the gun. It was only a moment, but I was terrified. And so was Bernard. I thought they were going to kill *us*."

CHAPTER EIGHT

Revenge!

Just after dinner, when were drinking coffee, the Vicar paid us a visit. I was shocked by his appearance. He had aged much more than I would have expected in only eight years.

"Something will *have* to be done!" he announced to us all. "And I mean, soon. We have done our best for these Children, but now they must be made to obey the law like the rest of us."

"We talked about these things years ago," Zellaby said. "That's why the Freemans came to help. But they couldn't find any way to control them. And I don't see how we can either."

"Almost everybody is meeting at the pub tonight," Mr Leebody said. "These deaths have been very difficult to bear. I wish there was something we could do, before it's too late. What *are* these Children? They look like human beings, but they do not act like them. I… "

He stopped speaking as he heard loud voices in the hall. Mrs Brant appeared in the doorway. She ran up to Mr Leebody and caught hold of his arm.

"Oh sir, you must come," she gasped. "They're all going up to Midwich Grange. They're going to burn it down! You must come and stop them, Vicar. Please hurry. They want to burn the Children."

As Mr Leebody left with her, we decided to follow them. But Angela shut the door and would not let us through.

"You must call the police, Gordon," she insisted. "They might kill you if you go up there."

"But this is important," Zellaby insisted. "We know what the Children can do with one person. I want to see if they can make a whole crowd turn round and go away."

"Nonsense!" Angela said. "That's not their way, and you know it. If it was, they would have simply made Jim Pawle stop his car and they'd have made David Pawle fire the second bullet into the air. They always fight back."

"You're right, Angela," Zellaby said.

"Now ring the police – and ask for ambulances as well," she said. "If you don't, I will."

"Angela, my dear," he said. "I am one of the few people the Children know. They're my friends…"

"Gordon," Angela interrupted. "You know quite well that the Children have *no* friends."

The Chief Constable came to question us the next morning. "It was a terrible sight," he said. "One woman and three men died. Eight men and five women were taken to hospital, including the Vicar. Everybody started to fight everybody else. But why, that's what I don't understand. Why *did* you call the police, Mr Zellaby?"

"Mrs Brant told us the villagers were going to burn down the school," he replied.

"So you mean that decent ordinary men and women marched on a school full of children, their own children, intending to set fire to them? You didn't think of asking questions. You just called the police?"

"Yes," Angela replied coldly.

"But there was no sign that they had tried to burn it," the Chief Constable replied, rubbing his head. "They were just fighting each other. It doesn't make sense." He stared at us all. "I'd heard there was something strange at Midwich!" he said.

CHAPTER NINE

Trapped

In the village, about ten women were waiting at the bus stop. They were going to visit their injured relatives in hospital. At last, the bus arrived. Miss Latterly, first in the queue, tried to step up onto the bus. But her feet would not leave the ground. The next woman tried to board and the same thing happened. Miss Latterly turned round and caught sight of one of the Children sitting opposite the bus stop, watching them. She walked over to him.

"I want to visit my friend in hospital," she said.

The boy shook his head.

"Haven't you done enough harm, you monsters!" Miss Latterly cried. "All we want to do is visit our friends who have been hurt because of you all! Haven't you *any* human feelings?"

Some of the women looked frightened. Some glared angrily at the boy. But nobody tried to get onto the bus and it moved off.

Mr Leebody's niece, Polly, was driving Mrs Leebody to see her husband in hospital. Just outside Midwich, she was forced to stop the car. Polly looked around her. One of the Children was sitting near the hedge, watching them.

"Are *you* doing this?" Polly asked her angrily.

The girl nodded. "You can't go." she said.

"Don't annoy her, Polly," her aunt said. "Wasn't last night a lesson for us all?"

Polly said no more. She glared at the child in the hedge. Then they drove back to Midwich in silence.

The Chief Constable decided to interview one of the Children, a boy called Eric, to find out what had happened. Bernard Westcott took him up to Midwich Grange.

"There was serious trouble last night, Eric," the Chief Constable began. "People are saying that you and the others had something to do with it. What do you say to that?"

"We had to defend ourselves," Eric replied. "We could have sent them away, but we made them fight each other so that they wouldn't come back."

"How did you make them?" the Chief Constable asked.

"It's too difficult to explain," Eric said. "I don't think you would understand."

"Your attitude is monstrous, Eric," the Chief Constable said. "Aren't you sorry for killing and injuring all those people?"

"One of them shot us yesterday," Eric replied. "Now we have to defend ourselves. The law only punishes after the wrong has been done. As you have not understood, I shall put it more plainly. If anybody tries to hurt us, we shall defend ourselves again."

The Chief Constable stared at Eric, speechless. Then he shouted at him angrily. Suddenly, the Chief Constable's mouth went slack and he began to talk nonsense. He tried to move, but he couldn't. He slid onto the floor and lay there screaming until he was sick.

"He is not hurt," Eric said. "He wanted to frighten us. So I have to show him what it is like to be frightened."

Eric turned and left the room. Bernard came back to Kyle Manor, white and trembling.

"The Chief Constable will be a broken man for the rest of his life," he muttered. "Those Children do not know their own strength."

"We do not seem to have realised that the Children are a danger to us humans," Zellaby said. "Yet they already realise that *we* are a danger to them."

"But they have not been violent up to now," Bernard replied.

"Does the government seriously accept that these Children are invaders?" I asked him.

"We do," Bernard told me. He hesitated. "And we have evidence to prove it. Midwich was not the only place to have a Dayout."

"So there *are* other groups of Children like ours!" Zellaby said. "Where?"

"There was a Dayout in Australia," Bernard replied, "but for some unknown reason, all the babies died after birth. Another was in an Eskimo settlement in Northern Canada. All the babies were left in the cold to die. There will have been others that we don't know about. Except for the one in Russia. The Children survived. We felt that if Russia had a group of child geniuses… "

"Then we should have one, too," Zellaby said.

"Their Children no longer exist," Bernard explained. "The village was blown up."

"You mean… *everybody* there?" Angela asked.

Bernard nodded. "They couldn't tell the villagers in case the news leaked out to the Children," he replied. "Now the Russian Government has begged other countries to do the same. They feel these Children are a threat to the human race."

"When did this happen?" Zellaby asked.

"Last week," Bernard replied.

"So that's what made them more violent," Zellaby said thoughtfully. "But how, I wonder, did *our* Children know?"

CHAPTER TEN

Saving Midwich

Bernard decided to go back to Midwich Grange after lunch. He met two of the Children staring up into the sky. As Bernard watched with them, he saw a jet plane flying away from the village. Its crew had ejected with parachutes. The Children looked at each other and smiled.

"Somebody is going to be very annoyed when that aircraft crashes," Bernard said. "Couldn't you just have turned the pilot back?"

"We *could* have killed everybody on it," the girl said.

"It's like last night," Bernard continued. "There was no need to kill people. It only makes us hate you."

The boy turned his golden eyes towards Bernard. "Sooner or later, you will try to kill us," he said. "That is why we have to protect ourselves. We do not like aeroplanes flying over us. They might kill us."

Bernard trembled as he listened. This nine year old boy was talking to him like an adult. "Are you Eric?" he asked.

"No," the boy replied. "I am Joseph. But now I am all of us. I want to say this. It doesn't matter whether you hate us or not. One day, you will *have* to kill us. If you don't, the human race is finished. It's already happened in Russia."

"So you know about that?" Bernard asked.

"Yes, of course," the boy replied.

"If we live, we shall dominate you," the girl said. "We are safe as long as you are trying to reach a decision. Some of your government will think it wrong to kill us in cold blood."

"Now we want to talk to you about something else," the boy said.

At the same time, I was taking a walk with Gordon Zellaby towards the woods when we discovered that we could not go any further. One of the Children was sitting in a tree above our path, eating a large bullseye sweet. Zellaby protested and we were allowed to walk on.

"Do you think the rest of the Children are enjoying that sweet?" Zellaby asked. "It's strange. I sometimes go up to the school to show them films. Now if one boy and one girl came to look, they would all enjoy it. But every child comes. I suppose they want to see it with their own eyes."

We met Bernard on his way back from Midwich Grange.

"How did you get on?" Zellaby asked him.

"The Children's only wish is to survive," Bernard replied. "They do not want to attack us. They have asked for aircraft to take them somewhere where they can live in peace. I shall put their request to my department. I saw what they did to the Chief Constable. They could make life very unpleasant for us all if I do not try."

"The government should act for the good of its people,"

Zellaby said. "It should destroy the Children. It is a pity. In the last nine years I have become rather fond of them." He stopped and looked around him at Midwich sitting quietly in the afternoon sun. "But I should be sorry to see all this destroyed, too."

***

"My dear," Gordon Zellaby said to his wife. "If you are going into Trayne this morning, would you bring back one of those large jars of bullseye sweets? I want to take them to the Children tonight."

"Nobody can leave the village," she complained. "You know that, Gordon. And if you are planning to show your film at Midwich Grange, I protest. The Children have killed *six* people and hurt a lot more. They could do the same to us at any time. Why are you defending them?"

"I'm not, my dear," he replied. "They have made a mistake because they are young. They know they will have to fight for their lives one day and they have done it too soon. Anyway, they have lifted their ban on leaving the village. I said I would cancel my film if they didn't. They're anxious and nervous at the moment. So they agreed."

For the rest of the day, Angela tried to persuade her husband not to go to the school that evening. But he insisted. I offered to help him with the heavy equipment. Before he left, Gordon Zellaby kissed Angela and stroked her face.

"Gordon…" she began. "I'm afraid of the Children now."

"You don't need to be, my dear," he replied. "I know what I'm doing."

We set off. As soon as everything was ready for the film show, Gordon asked me a last favour – to go back and spend the evening with Angela because she was so anxious. I agreed. She was sitting by the open window when I arrived.

"I don't trust the Children, Richard," she said. "Ever since they made their mothers come back here. They don't care what happens to us."

"Try not to worry," I reassured her. "They have already talked to Bernard. Perhaps he…" I stopped speaking. A bright flash, like lightning, lit up the sky and the house shook. Then there was silence. I ran into the garden. Above the trees, in the direction of Midwich Grange, I could see a white and red glare.

Midwich Grange had been blown to pieces – and Gordon Zellaby with it.

"That's why his boxes of equipment were so heavy!" I thought sadly.

I found Angela in Zellaby's study, at his desk, her face in her hands. A breeze blew a piece of paper from the desk to the floor. As I put it back next to Angela, I caught sight of a few lines in the middle, in Zellaby's handwriting: "…*if you want to keep alive in the jungle,*" he had written, "*you must live by the rules of the jungle. Forgive me, my dear…"*